Princess Katie's Kittens

Princess Katie's Kittens

☆

Collect all the kittens!

Pixie at the Palace

Bella at the Ball

Poppy and the Prince

Suki in the Snow

☆

PrincessKatiesKittens.co.uk

Princess Katie's Kittens

Ruby and the Royal Baby

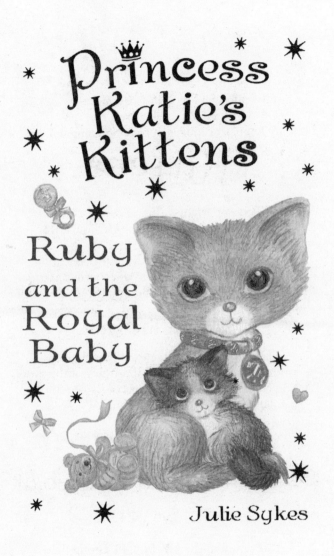

Julie Sykes

PICCADILLY PRESS

For Fiona Graham

First published in Great Britain in 2013
by Piccadilly Press
A Templar/Bonnier publishing company
Deepdene Lodge, Deepdene Avenue,
Dorking, Surrey, RH5 4AT
www.piccadillypress.co.uk

A catalogue record for this book is available
from the British Library

ISBN: 978 1 84812 352 6 (paperback)

1 3 5 7 9 10 8 6 4 2

Printed in the UK by CPI Group,
Croydon, CR0 4YY
Cover design by Simon Davis
Cover illustration by Sue Hellard

Chapter 1

Exciting News

Princess Katie and her best friend Becky were walking back from a riding lesson at the royal stables.

'I'm hungry. Miss Blaze worked us hard today,' said Becky.

Katie's stomach rumbled as if in agreement.

Becky giggled. 'It's ages until lunchtime. Let's find Mum and ask if we can have some cookies before we go and play with the kittens.'

'Good idea,' said Katie.

Mrs Philips, Becky's mum, was the royal housekeeper. She made the best cookies in the whole kingdom of Tula.

A parakeet screeched as Katie and Becky

hurried through the palace grounds. They walked under the arch of cherry trees, sidestepping a peacock pecking at a fallen cherry. At the stone staircase that led up the tiered lawns, Katie broke into a run.

'Race you to the top,' she called.

It was very close but Becky's foot touched the top step a fraction before Katie's.

'I won!' she said, collapsing on the grass.

'Well done,' said Katie. She was about to fall on the grass next to Becky when she saw her dad, the king, waving from the patio doors of the family lounge.

Katie waved back, but the king came outside and called both girls over.

Becky got up quickly and brushed the grass from her jodhpurs.

'Your dad looks very serious,' she said.

As they entered the lounge from the garden Katie was surprised to see her little brother, Alfie, perched on the edge of an armchair. The queen was sitting on a settee.

'Sit down, girls,' the king commanded.

'Are we in trouble?' asked Katie, as she sat cross-legged on the floor.

'Not unless there's something you haven't told me,' the king said, winking at Becky. His mouth stretched into a huge smile. 'Your mum and I have exciting news to share. We're having a baby. Katie and Alfie, you're going to have a new baby brother or sister.'

'That's *very* exciting!' Katie leapt up, ran to the queen and hugged her.

'So you're not just getting fat then,' said Alfie, joining in with Katie's hug.

'Alfie!' Katie tried not to giggle. In a stern voice she said, 'That's not polite.'

'But her tummy's huge,' said Alfie. 'I thought it was all the chocolate she keeps eating.'

The queen turned red.

'It's true,' laughed the king. 'Your mum has been eating a lot of chocolate recently – chocolate with cheese!'

'Eww!' Alfie pulled a face.

'I know, but I can't help it,' said the queen, joining in with the laughter. 'Sometimes when  you have a baby, it makes you do funny things. Last week I put my best tiara in the laundry basket by mistake. I keep feeling sick too, but chocolate and cheese makes me feel better.'

'I'd better ask Mum to keep lots in then,' said Becky.

'I've already asked her.' The queen tapped a china pot on the small table next to her. 'Chocolate and cheese, anyone?'

Katie, Becky and Alfie hastily shook their heads.

'Where's the new baby going to sleep?' asked Alfie.

'In the royal nursery,' the queen answered. 'It'll need a makeover first. It hasn't been used for years.'

'I had the nursery last,' said Alfie. 'I can't wait for the new baby to arrive. I won't be the youngest any more.'

The king patted Alfie's shoulder. 'You'll be the big brother.'

Alfie stuck out his chest. 'Can I go to bed at the same time as Katie?'

'No,' said the king. 'You can go to bed at

that time when you're nine, like Katie.'

'Watch it, shrimp,' teased Katie. 'You're still my *little* brother.'

Alfie put his head on one side. A huge smile spread over his face. 'So, I'll be a big brother and a little brother,' he said. 'I like it!'

'Can we help with the nursery make-over?' asked Katie.

'You certainly can,' said the queen. 'Mrs Philips is up there now, making a list of what needs to be done.'

'Let's go and tell the kittens about the new baby before we go to the nursery,' said Katie as she and Becky left the room.

Princess Katie told her kittens everything. They were brilliant listeners and she was sure they understood her.

When the girls reached
the boot room, where
the kittens slept, they
all rushed over.

'Hello Pixie, hello Poppy, hello Suki.'
Katie bent to stroke the tabby, the
tortoiseshell and the little white kitten, all
pushing at her leg. 'Hello Bella and
Pebbles,' she added as the black and white

kitten and the ginger one nudged the other
leg. 'Where's Tilly?'

'Here,' said
Becky, as a
silver-grey
and white
kitten jumped
out of the
king's walking
boot.
With the
kittens
gathered
around her, Katie told them about the new
baby. Then she gave them a fishy biscuit each
from the treats jar, to celebrate the good news.

'Next stop: the nursery,' said Katie,
putting the treats back in the cupboard.

Tilly, the silver-grey kitten with the four white paws, swallowed the last mouthful of her fishy biscuit. It was so tasty she could eat another two at least. But Princess Katie had put the jar away and she was walking towards the door. Tilly ran after her. 'Wait,' Tilly squeaked.

Katie was so excited about the new baby that she didn't notice the little cat follow them out of the room. On silent paws the kitten followed Katie and Becky along the wide hall. She was glad they took the spiral staircase to go upstairs and not the lift – that made her tummy go funny.

At the top of the stairs the girls walked along the corridor and went into the room at the end. Tilly stood in the doorway and peered inside. The room was bright and sunny but it hadn't been used for a long time. The air smelt old and dusty. Tilly's nose twitched with displeasure but curiosity got the better of her.

She followed Katie and Becky into the room where Mrs Philips was writing in a notebook. A ray of sunlight sliced through the window and onto the floor. Tilly pounced, her paws sliding through the light and sinking into the carpet. It was so soft, Tilly had a sudden urge to roll. She flipped onto her back and rocked from side to side. That felt good! Tilly nuzzled her face on the floor, loving the soft, bouncy feel of the carpet. She rolled again, then stretched out in an extra sunny patch in the middle of the room. It was the perfect place for a nap.

'Oh no you don't!'

A shadow fell over Tilly. She stared up, lazily. Mrs Philips stared back at her. Firmly but gently, she scooped Tilly up until they were face to face. Tilly tried to wriggle free but it was impossible.

Mrs Philips carried her to the door where she put her down. 'Shoo,' she said, clapping her hands. 'Kittens are *not* allowed in the nursery.'

Chapter 2

🐾

Cheese and Chocolate

The door shut with a bang. Tilly stared up at it indignantly. That wasn't very friendly. Why couldn't she stay? She glared at the closed door, then stalked along the hall towards the stairs. She passed a tall window, with long green curtains. The curtains rustled as she brushed by. Tilly spun round and cuffed them. The curtains billowed out and Tilly batted them away. It was such fun. She jumped and pounced at the curtains for ages, until at last she was worn out.

She stared up at the window ledge. It was wide and sunny – the perfect place for a rest. If she waited here, then Princess Katie might carry her back to the boot room.

Tilly bunched her muscles, wiggled her bottom and sprang. She landed neatly in the middle of the windowsill. She turned so that she could see the nursery door.

That was better! She was very tired now. Tilly settled down, with her head on her paws, to wait for Katie.

Princess Katie had been surprised to see Tilly in the nursery.

'Sorry, Mrs Philips, Tilly must have followed us out of the boot room. We'd better take her back.'

On her way to the door, Katie stopped to pick up a brochure from the table. 'Is this the paint chart? What colour is the nursery going to be?' she asked.

'The queen hasn't seen the chart yet. It only came today,' said Mrs Philips.

'Shall I take it to her?' asked Katie.

'That would be very helpful,' said Mrs Philips, gratefully. 'There's so much work to do here.'

Katie opened the chart as she left the room with Becky. 'Look at all the different shades of pink. That's my favourite, there.'

'Mine too!' exclaimed Becky. 'It's called candyfloss.'

Katie and Becky had their noses buried in the paint chart. They didn't notice Tilly, curled up asleep on the window ledge. Katie forgot all about the kitten as she went to find the queen.

The queen was in the lounge, flicking through a catalogue of baby toys while dipping into the tub of chocolate and cheese. She was pleased with the paint chart. 'I'll have a look at it now. Mr Palette is keen to get started with the painting.'

The toy catalogue gave Katie an idea. 'Let's make the new baby a present,' she suggested to Becky.

'Yes, let's!' said Becky. 'It should be something soft and cuddly.'

'A blanket!' Katie's eyes shone. 'We could ask Mrs Snippet for knitting needles and wool.'

Mrs Snippet was the royal dressmaker. They found her in the sewing room where she was measuring Alfie for a new pair of trousers. When Katie told her about the blanket, Mrs Snippet was relieved that Katie hadn't come to ask for some new clothes.

'I'm very busy,' she said. 'Alfie keeps growing. So does the queen, and I've got to make lots of outfits for the new baby too.'

Mrs Snippet went to the tall cupboard in the corner of the room. She opened the doors and Katie's eyes went round. The shelves were full of wool. 'Look at all the different colours,' she gasped. 'It looks like there's a rainbow in your cupboard.'

It took Katie and Becky ages to decide which colour to use for the new blanket. They both liked the sparkly pink wool best but Alfie pulled a face when they showed him.

'You can't use that,' he said. 'The baby might be a boy.'

'Boys can have pink things too,' said Katie.

'No, they can't,' said Alfie firmly.

'The blue's nice,' said Becky.

Alfie nodded approvingly. 'I like the blue. It's a boy's colour.'

'Blue is for girls and boys,' Katie told him.

Mrs Snippet reached into the cupboard and pulled out a ball of yellow wool. 'How about this one?' she suggested.

'That's lovely!' said Katie.

'It reminds me of fluffy chicks,' said Becky.

'It looks like sunshine,' said Alfie.

Princess Katie stroked the wool. 'It's very soft.'

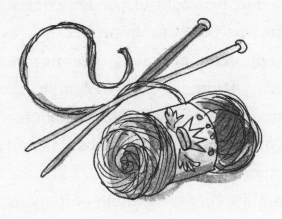

Mrs Snippet rummaged in a drawer for knitting needles. 'Would you like a set too, Alfie?'

'No, thanks,' said Alfie. 'I'm going to clean up my old mobile and give that to the baby instead. It's a space one, with rockets and stars.'

Alfie hurried off to look for his old mobile. Katie and Becky sat on the floor of the sewing room with a set of knitting needles each and two balls of yellow wool. Katie's tongue peeped out from her lips as she concentrated on making her first row of stitches. 'Knitting's *much* harder than I remember it being when I learnt it at school. It's going to take ages to make a blanket at this rate.'

'You'll soon get the hang of it again,' said

Mrs Snippet. 'If you each knit some squares, then I'll help you piece them together to make one big blanket.'

'Thank you,' said Katie.

By lunchtime, Katie and Becky had both knitted a tiny square of blanket.

'I'm so hungry,' said Becky, as she carefully speared the wool with her knitting needles, to stop her work from slipping off and unravelling. 'We forgot to ask Mum for cookies.'

Katie clapped a hand to her mouth. 'And we forgot to take Tilly back to the boot room.'

Becky frowned. 'I don't remember seeing her outside the nursery. Perhaps she found her own way back.'

'She might have. The kittens are much bigger. They're getting good at finding their way around now they're not shut up in the boot room all the time.'

Katie and Becky went to the boot room to look for Tilly. As they opened the door, Pixie ran past with a toy mouse. Bella, Poppy and Suki chased after him. Pebbles pounced out from behind a chair, snatched the mouse from Pixie and ran away. Pixie,

Bella, Poppy and Suki gave chase.

'One, two, three, four, five,' counted Becky. 'Tilly's not here so she must have either gone out into the garden or she's still outside the nursery.'

The outside door in the boot room had recently been fitted with a cat flap, so that the kittens could go out into the gardens whenever they wanted to.

Katie checked outside but Tilly wasn't

there. She glanced at her watch. 'There's just time to go and find her before lunch.' She left her knitting on top of the cupboard that held the cat treats, and ran upstairs to the nursery.

Chapter 3

Fun and Games

Tilly woke suddenly. She yawned and stretched out her paws. The front ones reached over the edge of the windowsill. Tilly stared at them in surprise. She must be getting bigger. There used to be plenty of room for her to sleep on the palace windowsills. She sat up and gave her face and the backs of her ears a quick wash, then she leapt to the floor. The nursery door was still shut. Tilly pushed it with her paw. It didn't open and it was very quiet inside. She pricked up her ears and listened at the door, but she couldn't hear anything. The room must be empty. So where was Princess Katie? Tilly went to look for her.

As she reached the bottom of the stairs she heard voices coming her way. She stopped, one white paw in the air. Her tail went stiff and her ears

twitched as she listened. Katie's voice floated along the corridor.

'Prrrip!' squeaked Tilly, as she ran to meet Princess Katie.

Katie and Becky rounded the corner and saw Tilly trotting towards them.

'There you are, you cheeky kitten.' Katie's breath huffed out in relief. She scooped Tilly up and cuddled her.

Tilly nuzzled Katie's cheek.

'Ooh! Your whiskers tickle,' said Katie.

A gong sounded loudly.

'Lunch!' Katie held Tilly away from her face. 'I'd better hurry or I'll be late.'

'Princesses are never late,' teased Becky, putting on a deep voice that sounded like the king.

They raced to the boot room and Katie opened the door a crack. Becky held back the other kittens while Katie put Tilly inside. Tilly squeaked with indignation as Katie closed the door.

'Sorry, kitten. I'll come and play with you soon.' Katie said goodbye to Becky, who was having lunch with her mum, then ran along to the dining room, stopping only to wash her hands in the cloakroom and smooth down her hair.

The king was just sitting down at the table as Katie burst into the room. She leapt onto her chair half a second before the king sat on his. He looked at his watch and frowned, but there was a twinkle in his eye. 'Busy morning?' he asked.

'Very,' said Katie, taking two prawn sandwiches from the plate the butler offered her. 'Becky and I are making a present for the new baby.'

'How lovely! What are you making?' the queen asked.

'It's a secret,' said Katie mysteriously.

'I'm giving the baby a present too, but that's not a secret,' said Alfie. 'I'm repairing my old mobile.'

'Alfie's painting the rockets green and the stars silver,' said Katie, taking a bite from her sandwich.

Alfie paused, with a tuna sandwich halfway to his mouth. His eyes widened in surprise. 'How did you know that?'

'You have silver and green paint

blobs on your nose,' giggled Katie. 'Have you decided what colour to paint the nursery yet, Mum?'

The queen nodded. 'I've chosen two colours. Buttercup yellow and silver.'

Katie's eyes sparkled with excitement. The room would be a perfect match for the blanket she was knitting with Becky. She gave Alfie a knowing look and he grinned back at her.

'That's a good choice,' she said as she took a sip of her peach juice.

Tilly couldn't believe it when the boot room door shut behind her.

'Not again!' she said crossly. Why did everyone keep shutting her in or out? Surely she was getting big enough to look after herself?

Bella batted a ball to Tilly. 'Come and play with me,' she called. Tilly watched the ball roll towards her. Her paws twitched as she reached out and batted the ball back. The ball whizzed straight past Bella, hit the wall and shot off in a different direction. Tilly and Bella skittered after it. Bella reached it first and knocked the ball under a chair. Both kittens dived for it and ended up in a tangle.

Bella was on her paws first and hit the
ball across the room. Tilly raced after it. It
was such fun chasing the ball that Tilly soon
forgot she was cross.

Bella
whacked the
ball extra hard.
It bounced
across the floor
and landed in
the queen's
tennis shoe,
then rolled into
the toes.

Bella jumped in to get it but she was too
big to fit. She stretched out her paw,
wiggling it to try and reach the ball.

Tilly watched Bella but after a while she

got bored and wandered off. As she passed
the treats cupboard, Tilly noticed something
long and yellow
hanging from it.
She stretched her front
paws up and sniffed it.
The string thing was
soft and fluffy and
moved when she
breathed. Tilly
cuffed it with her
paw. It swung to
and fro. Tilly batted
it again. Her claw
caught in the thread.
She shook her paw but the yellow
thread was stuck there. As Tilly
walked away she felt something drag after

her. There was a sudden loud clatter. Tilly spun round and hissed as a ball of the yellow stuff and two metal sticks fell from the cupboard on top of her.

'Wool!' squeaked Poppy, galloping over. 'I love wool.' Tilly liked the squishy yellow wool too. She nudged her face against the small knitted square. It was so soft. The metal sticks were fun and made a clattering noise when she pushed them.

Tilly and Poppy teased the wool until the yellow square slid off the needles and unravelled. Tilly sighed. The game had been fun while it lasted. She gave the wool a final pat with her paw then went to find something else to play with.

Chapter 4

Oh Tilly!

After lunch Katie went back to the nursery to see if Mrs Philips had finished writing up her list of things to do. Becky was there, talking to Mr Palette. The royal painter was slapping bright white paint onto the walls.

Katie's heart sank. 'Has mum changed her mind about the colour?' she asked. 'I thought she wanted yellow and silver.'

Mr Palette pointed at the paint pot with his brush. 'This is undercoat,' he said with a smile. 'Painting a room is a bit like getting dressed. You have to put on lots of layers. The undercoat goes on first. Mrs Philips has gone to the shop to buy the yellow and silver paint.'

'Can we help with the painting?' asked Princess Katie.

'I don't see why not,' said Mr Palette. He rummaged in his workbag for two more paintbrushes and two sets of overalls. He winked as he handed them over. 'You'd better put these on. A princess and her friend mustn't get paint on their clothes,' he said.

Mr Palette showed Katie and Becky where he wanted them to paint. It was great fun dipping the brushes into the paint pot then slathering it over the wall. By the time Mrs Philips returned with the coloured paint, Katie and Becky had painted the lower half of their wall.

'Thank you, girls,' said Mr Palette. 'That's helped me out a lot.'

'We haven't finished yet,' said Becky, eyeing the triangular stepladder that Mr Palette was using to reach the high bits.

'That's enough painting for today,' said Mrs Philips. 'I need you girls to help me choose a new cot for the baby, if you'd like to?'

'Yes, please,' said Katie. She put her brush

in Mr Palette's painting tray to avoid getting paint on the carpet, and hung her overall on the stepladder.

Mrs Philips pulled her laptop out of her bag and switched it on. 'I found this great site on the internet. It's got everything a royal baby could ever need.'

Katie and Becky crowded round the computer screen. Katie's eyes widened as the page loaded. 'I never knew there were so many different types of cot,' she said. All of the cots were made of wood. Some had bars and some had solid side panels.

'The bars are funny – they make the cot look like a cage,' said Becky with a giggle.

'Yes, but they also allow the baby to see out,' said Mrs Philips. 'The new baby will be unable to sit up at first. If a cot has bars, the

baby can see what's happening in the room.'

'Let's get a cot with bars,' said Katie, decisively. 'Imagine how awful it would be not to be able to see your own room.'

'The queen wants a white cot, to match the rest of the furniture,' said Mrs Philips. She clicked on the words *white* and *bars* to narrow her search. The computer flashed and a new page loaded, showing only white cots with bars.

'I like that one,' said Katie, pointing at the screen. 'The one with the unicorn carved into the headboard? I like that one too,' said Becky.

Mrs Philips scrolled down the page. Some of the headboards were plain, one had jungle animals carved on it, one had balloons and another had teddy bears.

'The unicorn is lovely,' Mrs Philips agreed. 'I'd better check with the queen first. If she likes it then I'll place an order. The cot will need a mattress too. Hmm, now, what size?'

Katie and Becky soon lost interest as Mrs Philips scrolled through pages of mattresses.

They moved away and watched Mr Palette put the first stroke of yellow on the walls.

'It's going to look gorgeous,' said Katie, standing back to admire the colour.

'We'd better get on with our blanket,' said Becky, 'or it won't be ready in time!'

Becky had to go back to her room in the west tower to collect her knitting. At first Katie couldn't remember where she'd left hers.

'You put it on the cupboard in the boot room,' Becky reminded her.

'Of course!' said Katie. 'I'll meet you in the garden. It's too sunny to knit indoors.'

Katie dashed along to the boot room. She pushed open the door, then froze. Her knitting lay in ruins on the floor. Her heart thumped in her chest and she had to take a very deep breath to stop herself from crying.

Tilly was curled with one paw resting on a knitting needle. She meowed happily when she saw Katie.

'Oh Tilly,' Katie whispered. 'What have you done?'

She fell to her knees to examine the

damage. There was nothing left of her knitting and the wool was full of snags and knots. Katie bit her lip, determined to behave like a proper princess and not cry.

As she gathered up the wool and the needles, she suddenly remembered how Bella had once ruined the queen's new birthday dress. Mrs Snippet had fixed the dress for Mum – maybe she could help Katie fix the knitting? Katie hurried off to find the dressmaker.

Tilly wasn't surprised that Katie was dashing off again. Recently, she was always in a hurry. It would be fun to follow her to see where she was going.

In the hall, a maid came out of another

door pushing a vacuum cleaner. Tilly jammed her paws into the carpet and skidded to a halt. She hated the noisy vacuum cleaner that tried to gobble her up if she got too close.

Thankfully the vacuum cleaner was switched off, but by the time the maid had passed by, Katie had vanished.

Tilly put her head on one side to think. Katie had headed off in the same direction as earlier. Maybe she was going back to the sunny room.

Tilly had a good sense of direction and before long she was back at the nursery. The door was open. What luck! She went inside but the room was empty. Katie hadn't come here after all.

Tilly stared round in surprise. The room seemed different. Her nose twitched delicately. The musty smell had disappeared. The window was open and Tilly could smell the fresh outdoors. There was another smell too. It was quite strong and made her tummy feel funny.

The smell seemed to be coming from a tin on the carpet.

Tilly walked over to investigate. The tin was full of a creamy liquid. Tilly stuck her nose inside, hoping to find milk. The smell from the liquid made her whiskers twitch and her nose tremble. She pulled away quickly and stepped back into a large plastic tray.

'Eww!' There was liquid in the tray too. It definitely wasn't milk. It had a strong smell that Tilly didn't care for. She didn't like the way the liquid stuck to her paws either, but she wasn't prepared to lick it off. Tilly shook her paws delicately. Some of the liquid spun across the room. It splattered like raindrops on the carpet.

Tilly's paws were still covered in the

horrible liquid. Where was Katie? Tilly
wanted a cuddle and someone to help her
get clean again. She ran to
the door, leaving a trail
of yellow paw prints
in her wake.

Chapter 5

Thunder!

The weeks flew by and soon Katie and Becky were sitting on a large rug in the garden, in the shelter of an enormous striped sunshade. There was a tray between them, laden with a large jug of iced peach juice and two glasses with curly straws.

'Phew!' said Becky, pushing her curly

brown hair back from her face. 'It's far too hot for June.

Katie had tied back her long, blond hair with a piece of yellow wool. 'Make the most of it. Dad said we might get a storm soon,' she replied.

Becky held up her knitting. They had knitted lots of squares for the blanket now. 'Look how big the blanket is getting since we found out about the baby.'

'It's almost finished,' said Katie, holding her knitting up to compare it with Becky's.

'You've done more than me,' said Becky.

'That's only because Mrs Snippet did lots for me when Tilly ruined my first attempt,' said Katie generously.

'Troublesome Tilly!' said Becky.

'Tilly the Terror,' said Katie, in agreement. 'I was so upset when I discovered she'd spoilt my knitting. It was such a relief that Mrs Snippet could help me start again.'

'Tilly was in *big* trouble that day,' said Becky. 'Remember how she walked through the paint and put yellow paw prints on the nursery carpet?'

'How could I forget!' Even thinking about it made Katie feel wobbly inside. 'Your mum nearly exploded when she saw the mess. I thought she was going to make me give Tilly away.'

'She was very cross,' said Becky. 'She couldn't get the paint out of the carpet, so it was lucky that the queen decided to buy a new one to match the new paint.'

'Tilly's been very good since then,' Katie pointed out. 'I've been making sure that she keeps out of trouble. Mum won't let her stay if she keeps spoiling things.'

Becky put down her knitting. 'Speaking of kittens, we haven't played with them today. Shall we go and see what they're doing?'

Katie readily agreed. 'Good idea, my fingers are aching.'

They put their knitting in the family lounge – in a dresser drawer, where it would be safe from the kittens. Then they went along to the boot room. Only Tilly and Suki were there. Katie and Becky got out the ball with the bell in the middle and played a rolling game with them.

The kittens didn't wait for the ball to be rolled to them, but chased after it and batted it across the carpet with their paws.

After a bit, Becky fell on her hands and knees. 'Miaow,' she purred. 'Look at me. I'm a cat too.'

Katie joined in. Crawling along, she pushed the ball with her nose. It wasn't easy and she kept toppling over. Soon both girls could hardly breathe for laughing.

'That was fun,' said Katie, collapsing on the floor.

'It's made me thirsty. Let's go and get a drink,' said Becky.

Katie stood up. 'We'd better walk properly. Can you imagine what Dad would say if he sees me on all fours?'

'A princess must never behave like a

kitten,' both girls chorused.

As they walked to the kitchen, they saw a large lorry rumble past the window.

'That must be bringing the new baby things,' said Becky. 'Mum said everything was arriving today.'

'How exciting!' Katie's eyes sparkled. 'Let's go and see what the new cot looks like.'

They ran along to the back door and found the lorry parked in the courtyard. Two men were unloading boxes, while Mrs Philips ticked them off on a piece of paper.

'That's everything,' she said at last.

The men got back into the lorry and it drove away. Mrs Philips organised the palace staff to carry the boxes up to the nursery.

'Can we help?' Katie asked.

Mrs Philips gave them a small box each to carry.

'I wonder what's in here,' said Katie.

'Baby bedding, I think.' Mrs Philips smiled. 'Would you and Becky like to help me unpack?'

'Yes, please,' chorused Katie and Becky.

In the nursery the girls set about opening the parcels. 'This is just like Christmas,' said Becky, as she pulled a pretty silver lamp out of a box.

Katie was unpacking curtains. They were yellow with white ducks printed on

them. Mrs Philips stood on a stepladder to hang them.

'Aren't they sweet?' said Katie.

'And look,' said Becky, pulling a rug from a box. 'The ducks on this match the ones on the curtains.'

'That's to go by the cot,' said Mrs Philips. 'Put it on the floor, just there.'

There was a comfy chair for the queen to sit on when she was nursing the baby, and a stack of yellow and gold cushions to put on it. There was a clock with teddy bears for the wall and a set of silver photo frames.

Katie and Becky arranged them in size order, on the table with the lamp.

There was only one box left to unpack. Becky tore it open and Katie looked inside.

'Look,' she said, holding up a delicate white blanket. 'It's so tiny.'

'And soft.' Becky stroked the blanket.

'Your blanket is lovely too,' said Mrs Philips. 'We'll make the cot up now and when you've finished your blanket, it can go on top.'

'Really?' said Katie. 'Thank you!'

Mrs Philips unpacked the huge box with the cot in next.

'It's gorgeous,' said Katie, admiring the carved unicorn on the headboard. 'I can't wait for the baby to arrive.'

'It won't be long now,' said Mrs Philips,

with a smile. She lifted the new mattress into the cot, then made it up with crisp white sheets and two soft blankets.

'Phew!' said Becky. 'If this weather keeps up the baby won't need any blankets.'

'It is unusually warm,' Mrs Philips agreed.

'Dad says it's because there's a storm coming,' said Katie.

Mrs Philips glanced thoughtfully at the window. 'I must remember to shut that later. I've been leaving it open to get rid of the paint smell.'

Katie wasn't surprised when a loud clap of thunder woke her in the night. She watched the lightning flash through a chink in the curtains and counted the seconds until she heard the boom of thunder. Rain splattered against the window and made the glass rattle. After a while, Katie pulled the duvet up to her nose. It was cosy lying there, listening to the storm. She was glad the kittens didn't go out at night. She imagined them curled up together in their basket and soon she was fast asleep herself.

Tilly jumped as a loud boom tore the air. What was that? Her fur stood on end and her tail went stiff.

'It's all right,' said Pixie. He opened an eye, then closed it again, sleepily. 'It's only thunder, it won't hurt you.'

'I don't like it,' squeaked Tilly.

'Shh, or you'll wake the others. If you go back to sleep then you won't hear it,' murmured Pixie, sensibly.

Tilly closed her eyes and tried to block out the noise of the thunder. It didn't work. She lay trembling in the cat basket while the other kittens slept on, but after a while she needed the toilet. She tried not to think about it but it was no good. Tilly knew she'd have to get up and go.

There was another loud crack of thunder. Tilly jumped up. Her fur stood out, like the bristles on a hairbrush. If she was quick she could get outside, go to the toilet and be back indoors before the lightning and thunder started up again.

Tilly scrambled out of bed and ran to the cat flap. She pushed it open and jumped outside. As she crouched under a bush there was a huge flash of light that seemed to tear the sky apart. The crack of thunder that followed made Tilly's ears sing.

The rain beat on her back as she tore across the wet grass to the cat flap. But it didn't open. Tilly banged against it but in her panic she couldn't get it to work.

Tilly's heart thumped like a charging rhino as she ran round the palace, looking for another way in. All the doors were shut and locked. She'd almost given up hope of finding a way indoors when she noticed an open window, on the first floor of one of the towers. Roses curled up the wall.

Tilly timidly put a paw on a branch. It was strong enough to take her weight. Another flash of lightning illuminated the sky

and Tilly shot up
the rose bush.
She was soaked
to the skin and
covered in leaves
and wet petals
when she reached
the top. Tilly
squeezed in
through the
window. Her nose
twitched and even
before her eyes had
adjusted to the

dark room she knew where she was. Tilly
sighed with relief.

The room was full of new furniture.
Tilly stared around and found the perfect

place to rest. In two leaps she bounced from the windowsill, to the chest of drawers, and into the new cot. She turned in a circle, kneading the blanket with her claws. The soft wool brought back distant memories of her mum. It felt safe here. Tilly curled up in the middle of the blanket and fell asleep.

Chapter 6

❖

Tilly in Trouble

Katie woke early to see the sun pouring through a gap in her curtains. The palace gardens were still damp from the huge storm and raindrops sparkled in the grass. Katie dressed quickly. She'd planned to meet Becky in the nursery. Katie thought they had enough squares to sew together into a blanket but she wanted to measure the cot first, to make sure.

Katie ran down the spiral staircase and

threw open the boot-room door. 'Morning, kittens,' she called. Poppy and Pebbles ran over. 'Where is everyone? Are they out in the garden?' asked Katie, stroking each kitten on the head. She took six cat bowls from the cupboard and shook a portion of cat biscuits into each one. Next Katie refreshed the kittens' drinking water. She stuck her head out of the boot room door and called to the missing kittens to come and get their breakfast. She was in too much of a hurry to wait for them to appear though.

Katie and Alfie had their breakfast alone as the king was having a working breakfast in his office with his advisor. The queen was in her office too, dealing with her e-mail.

'My mobile's finished,' said Alfie, serving

up scrambled egg from a warm dish. 'Mrs Philips is going to hang it in the nursery today for me.'

Katie took some scrambled egg, two pieces of toast and a big mug of tea.

'Snap,' she said. 'Our blanket is almost finished too.'

After breakfast Katie went to the sewing room to ask Mrs Snippet for a tape measure. She met Becky and Mrs Philips on the way back and they walked to the nursery together.

'I'm looking forward to seeing your blanket,' said Mrs Philips, as they reached the top of the stairs.

A loud scream made everyone jump.

'Mum!' said Katie, her face turning white.

She raced down the hall to the nursery

and threw open the door.

'Get out,' shrieked the queen. 'Out, I say!'

Katie froze. Why was Mum shouting at her like that?

The queen began to cry. Mrs Philips rushed into the room. She marched over to the new cot.

She bent over
it and lifted
something up.

Katie
gasped.
'Tilly!
How
did
you
get
there?'

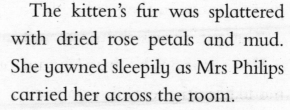

The kitten's fur was splattered with dried rose petals and mud. She yawned sleepily as Mrs Philips carried her across the room.

'Oh Tilly!' Katie stared in disbelief at the new cot. The white blankets were patterned with muddy paw prints. They were also covered with silver-grey cat hairs, grass, leaves and dried rose petals.

Tears ran down the queen's face. Katie put her arms round her and hugged her tightly. 'Don't worry,' she said. 'Mrs Philips will put it right. She's really good at fixing things.'

Katie crossed her fingers and hoped that even Mrs Philips could

put the room back as it had been.

The queen was too upset to be comforted though. The pregnancy made her very tearful. 'I don't *ever* want to see a cat in my nursery again,' she sobbed.

Mrs Philips handed Tilly over to Becky but the kitten was scared and struggled to get free. She gave a frightened squeak as she jumped out of Mrs Philips's arms and shot from the room.

The queen slammed the door to stop Tilly from coming back again. 'No cats in here,' she said firmly.

Mrs Philips patted the queen's arm. 'There, there,' she said kindly. 'Why don't you go and sit down

and I'll bring you a nice hot cup of tea.'

She turned to Becky and said quietly, 'Help the queen to the lounge, please, sweetheart.'

The queen wiped her eyes. 'Thank you, Mrs Philips.' She gave Katie a watery smile, then she tucked her arm in Becky's and allowed herself to be led away.

Mrs Philips turned to Katie when she'd gone. She scooped her up and gave her an enormous hug. 'Don't look so scared,' she said. 'Your mum's going to be fine. She just had a nasty shock.'

'I feel awful,' said Katie. 'I know exactly how Mum feels. I was so upset when Tilly ruined my knitting. Mum's normally quite calm, though. I've never seen her this upset. She must be really cross with Tilly and me.'

'You're mum's not cross with you,' Mrs Philips said gently. 'She's just had a fright finding Tilly in the cot. New babies are totally helpless. They're also very cuddly. If an animal, like Tilly, cuddles up to a baby then it might accidentally suffocate him or her. It's very important that the kittens don't come anywhere near the nursery on their own, when the baby has arrived.'

'Oh!' said Katie. 'So Mum's not cross about the mess then?'

Mrs Philips smiled. 'I expect she's very cross about the mess too, but she's not cross with you. If anyone is to blame then it's me. I forgot to shut the window last night. I'm going to make your mum a cup of hot tea and then I'll wash the blankets. From now on, we all have to be extra careful to make sure that Tilly and the other kittens stay out of the nursery. Otherwise they might be looking for a new home!'

Katie's heart sank to her toes. She couldn't let that happen! She'd have to watch the kittens every minute of the day.

After Mrs Philips left, Katie quickly measured the cot. She was still worried about her mum but she was even more worried about Tilly. The kitten had seemed terrified when she'd run from the room. With the measuring done, Katie hurried to the boot room to comfort her.

Not one of the kittens was indoors. Katie

stepped outside and found Pixie, Pebbles and Poppy strolling around on the grass. Bella was chasing a butterfly while Suki watched from the top of a low wall.

'Tilly,' called Katie. 'Tilly, where are you?'

As she was looking, Becky arrived with good news about the queen. 'Your mum is much happier now. She's reading a magazine, with a cup of tea and a plate of chocolate biscuits . . . and cheese.' Becky wrinkled her nose and Katie laughed.

'That's good. Now we just need to find Tilly. We have to keep her busy and away from the nursery.'

Katie and Becky searched the small fenced garden outside the boot room.

'She's not here,' said Katie.

'She must have climbed over the fence

again, like she did last night,' said Becky. 'Now the kittens are bigger it's going to be

impossible to keep
them in one place
unless we shut them
in the boot room.'

'They're too big to be shut in one room all
day,' said Katie. Her face creased with worry
lines. 'I remember shutting the nursery door,
but I think I'll just go and check, in case Tilly
has gone back there again.'

'She does like the nursery,' said Becky.

The girls ran upstairs. The nursery door
was tightly shut and Mrs Philips was inside
stripping the dirty bedding from the cot.

'I'll have this sorted in no time,' she
reassured Katie.

'What now?' asked
Becky as they left Mrs
Philips to her work.

'We'd better search the palace and the rest of the gardens,' said Katie. 'Tilly can't have gone far.'

Katie and Becky spent the whole morning looking for Tilly. They asked the palace staff to keep an eye out for her too. When the gong sounded for lunch, the kitten was still missing. Princess Katie pushed her pasta salad around her plate. It was one of her favourite meals but she wasn't at all hungry.

Chapter 7

Where Is Tilly?

When lunch was over Katie and Becky took their squares of yellow knitting along to the sewing room, to ask Mrs Snippet if she could help them turn their handiwork into a blanket. Mrs Snippet reminded them how to cast off first.

Casting off was usually Katie's favourite

part of knitting. She loved to see the item she'd spent so long creating drop off the knitting needles and become a finished piece of work. Today though, she was too distracted to enjoy the moment. Her mind kept wandering to Tilly and how scared the kitten had looked as she'd raced from the nursery.

'Please concentrate, Princess,' Mrs Snippet said gently. 'You've dropped a stitch. If you don't catch it then you'll have a hole in your blanket.'

'Poor baby!' said Becky.

Katie forced her mind back to her work.

Mrs Snippet helped the girls to pin the squares of blanket together, then gave them some thread and a needle to join them. Becky did half and Katie finished it off.

She
struggled
to keep her
mind on
the blanket
and kept
pricking
herself.

'Careful,'
said Becky.

'Sorry,'
said Katie.

Mrs Snippet found the girls some yellow silk with which to edge the blanket. It was very slippery and took ages to sew on. Katie could hardly contain her impatience as she stitched it in place.

At last the blanket was finished. Katie and

Becky held it up for Mrs Snippet to see.

'It's lovely!' declared the dressmaker. 'The silk edging gives it that extra special touch.'

Katie had to agree!

'I've got to press Alfie's trousers and the

new baby clothes. I could give the blanket a quick iron for you, then give it to Mrs Philips,' Mrs Snippet offered.

'Yes, please!' Katie wanted to take the blanket to the nursery so that it would be ready in time for the baby's arrival, but she was worried about Tilly and wanted to go and look for her too.

'Tilly can't be in the palace or we'd have found her by now,' she said to Becky as they left the sewing room.

'Then she must be in the grounds,' said Becky.

'The grounds are huge.' Katie looked thoughtful. 'We've got a riding lesson soon. Shall we ask Miss Blaze if we can hack around the gardens? Then we can look for Tilly at the same time.'

'That's a great idea,' said Becky.

Miss Blaze said that they could hack around the gardens, just so long as they didn't go on the grass. 'The king won't be pleased if he finds hoof prints on the lawns,' she added.

She left Katie and Becky in the yard, brushing down Misty and Honey, while she

went to get her own horse ready.

Misty and Honey looked lovely after they'd been groomed. Katie and Becky tacked the ponies up in saddles and bridles, then used the block in the yard to mount them.

'Ready?' asked Miss Blaze. She checked

the ponies' girths, to make sure they were fastened tightly around their tummies, before she mounted her horse.

Katie and Becky spent the rest of the afternoon riding around the palace grounds.

They searched the woods, the meadow around the lake and the formal gardens. They even walked the ponies around the maze! They saw plenty of red squirrels, parakeets and peacocks.

Then Katie spotted Tilly in the distance, heading towards the woods. She pushed Misty after her, but Tilly was too fast and soon Katie lost sight of her. Miserably she turned to Becky. 'What if Tilly's running away?'

'She isn't,' said Becky. 'She's probably sulking because the queen shouted at her. She'll come back when she's hungry.'

Becky sounded confident but her brown eyes were troubled. Katie wanted to believe her sensible friend, but she couldn't help thinking that Becky had only said that to make her feel better.

Soon after, Miss Blaze called out, 'Sorry, girls. It's time to take the ponies home.'

The knot in Katie's stomach tightened. What was Tilly doing in the woods and when would she come home?

Tilly was too frightened to think where she was going as she fled from the nursery. She raced down the spiral staircase, as if a pack of wolves was on her tail. She kept going along the wide palace hallways and only stopped when she'd run out of breath. Tilly slipped into a wood-panelled room. It had a huge floor-to-ceiling bookcase and a large desk covered with paper and pens. She crawled under the desk and stayed there until

her heart was beating normally again.

At last, she felt brave enough to investigate her new surroundings. Where was she? She didn't recognise it here. Tall doors led out into the palace gardens. One was open. The fresh air made Tilly's nose twitch. She went outside and found herself in a courtyard. Tilly settled down on a sunny patch of stone and began to clean herself.

Ages later, when she'd licked all the dried petals, strands of grass and lumps of mud from her fur, Tilly realised how hungry she was. She was about to try and find her way back to the boot room when she heard a noise.

Mouse!

Tilly sat up straight with her ears pricked. The noise came again, only now it didn't sound so mousey. Tilly's ears twitched as she tried to work out who was making the funny noise. It seemed to be coming from the other side of the wall.

Tilly trotted through the stone arch, then stopped to listen. There it was again – a high-pitched squeak.

Tilly wrinkled her nose, searching for a scent. The air was heavy with pollen but, when she breathed deeply enough, she could just identify something else. It was only faint, but very interesting.

Tilly followed it across the neatly mowed grass, under the fence and into the meadow beyond. The grass was longer here and

rustled as she passed through it. The scent was growing stronger.

Tilly crossed the meadow until she reached the woods on the other side. A fallen tree lay rotting on the ground, and either the tree was squeaking or there was something hidden in its trunk.

Tilly pushed her head inside to look. It took a moment for her eyes to adjust to the darkness. Her tail swished in surprise.

'Prrip!' she squeaked and she wriggled further into the tree.

Tilly stared. There in front of her was a tiny kitten. It was even smaller than she was, with matchstick-sized bones that poked through her rich, red and brown fur. The kitten's eyes seemed too large for her face, and glowed in the dark.

Tilly was overcome with an urge to protect the tiny cat. She squeezed up alongside her and began to lick her face. The kitten gave a sigh and nestled her thin body against Tilly's plumper one.

'I've lost my mummy,' she said with a sob.

'Hush! I'll look after you,' said Tilly, and she started to wash behind the kitten's ears.

Chapter 8

🐾

Two New Babies

It was almost bedtime and Princess Katie was just about to have a bath before she got into her pyjamas. She didn't feel tired, though. She'd spent most of the day worrying about Tilly.

The silver-grey kitten had only been seen once since she'd disappeared into the woods. The cook had tripped over her in the kitchen. She'd given her some leftover fish from lunchtime, but instead of eating it, Tilly had taken it outside. That was ages ago! Katie couldn't understand why Tilly had disappeared again. What ever was she up to?

A knock on the bedroom door made Katie almost jump out of her sparkly pink slippers.

'Come in,' she said, quickly recovering herself.

The door flew open and the king stood in the doorway.

'It's time,' he said. 'Your mum is ready to have her baby. I'm going with her to the hospital.'

The king gave Katie a hug, then ruffled her hair. 'Isn't this exciting? Very soon, you'll

have a new sister or brother. Mrs Philips is
going to keep an eye on you and Alfie
while we're at the hospital. She'll be up in a
moment to help you run your bath.'

The king gave
Katie one last
swift hug before
he left. Katie
stared at the
door as it closed.
A funny feeling
prickled her skin.
Excitement, she
decided, along
with a dose of
nerves. She was
used to Mum
and Dad staying

away from home. As King and Queen of Tula, they often went away, sometimes for weeks at a time and to a foreign country. This felt different though. Katie was a little anxious about Mum going to hospital.

There was another knock on the door and Mrs Philips came in.

'Are you all right, Katie? I expect you're a bit nervous, aren't you?'

'Yes, I am!' Katie exclaimed. She was pleased that Mrs Philips understood exactly how she was feeling.

'I've come to help you run a bath.' Mrs Philips started towards Katie's bathroom.

'Mrs Philips,' said Katie, hesitantly. 'I'm not very tired yet. I'm worried about Tilly. She hasn't been seen since the cook watched her go outside this afternoon. Please could I

have a look for
her, before I go
to bed?'

Mrs Philips
looked at
Katie. 'Oh,
sweetie. Try
not to worry
too much.
Tilly will be

back before it's dark. But if you're worried,
then how about you and Becky have a
quick look in the garden together?'

Katie's breath rushed out in relief. 'That
would be perfect.'

It was still very warm. Katie would have
enjoyed her evening stroll round the
gardens with Becky if it hadn't have been

for Tilly. Katie sighed, anxiously. It wasn't like Tilly to stay away from people for so long. She was the most timid of the kittens and never strayed far from the palace. Katie peered into the flowerbeds and under the bushes as she walked.

'It's nearly time to go back,' said Becky, with a glance at her watch.

Katie made a sad face. 'Let's walk as far as the next lamppost, then turn around.'

At night the palace gardens were lit by old-fashioned street lamps and coloured lights that hung from the trees and bushes. The lights hadn't come on yet, as it didn't get dark until very late in the summer. When they reached the next street lamp Katie leant her head against the cool metal pole. Becky stood silently next to her.

'Pardon?' said Becky, looking up.

Katie stared at her in surprise. 'I didn't say anything.'

'Oh! I thought you squeaked,' said Becky. 'Listen – there it is again.'

The girls stood very still and suddenly Katie heard the noise too. 'That's not a squeak, it's a miaow!'

She set off, running towards the noise, and there was Tilly coming along the path with a kitten even tinier than she was.

'Tilly, where have you been?' Katie cried. She stopped running, so as not to frighten the new kitten. Tilly bounced towards her then stopped, waiting for her new friend to catch up.

Katie and Becky crouched down to stroke Tilly and the strange kitten.

'Where have you come from?' asked Becky.

'She's either been abandoned or she's lost,' said Katie. 'Look how bony she is!'

Katie lifted the kitten up and stroked her red-brown fur. 'She doesn't have a collar so I expect she's been abandoned. I wonder what her name is?'

'Ruby,' said Becky, then she laughed. 'She's the same colour as rubies.'

'Ruby's a lovely name,' said Katie. 'I wonder if I'll be allowed to keep her.'

'I don't think she's yours to keep,' said Becky. She nodded at Tilly who was anxiously pushing against Katie's legs.

Suddenly Tilly reached up and put her front paws on Katie's knees as if she was about to climb up her in order to reach Ruby.

Becky laughed and picked Tilly up,

holding her
out so she
could see
Ruby. Tilly
swiftly licked
Ruby's nose
and the tiny
kitten
purred,
happily.

'That's
settled then,' said Katie.
'Having a tiny kitten to look after will keep
Tilly busy and stop her from getting into
any more trouble.'

Katie could hardly believe how happy she
was. She asked Mrs Philips if she could keep
Ruby and Mrs Philips said she thought that

the king and queen would agree to it. She also helped Katie to fence off a small area of the boot room for Tilly and Ruby to sleep in, while Ruby got used to the other five kittens.

Katie smiled as she settled down in her bed that night. With any luck tomorrow would be an even better day. Katie couldn't wait to meet her new brother or sister.

Katie bubbled with excitement as she and Alfie stood at the nursery door.

'Ready?' she asked.

Alfie nodded.

Katie knocked and her mother's voice called out quietly, 'Come on in.'

Katie held Alfie's hand as they crossed over the new carpet.

'Your mobile looks lovely,' she whispered.

Alfie's mobile, complete with green rockets and silver stars, hung over the royal cot.

'So does the blanket that you and Becky made,' Alfie replied.

Katie smiled with pleasure as she walked towards the cot. Her baby sister was tucked up under the yellow blanket.

The queen sat in a big armchair. She put her finger to her lips. 'Shh,' she whispered. 'Eliza's just fallen asleep.'

Katie and Alfie peeped through the cot bars at their new sister, Eliza.

'She's lovely,' sighed Katie. 'And so tiny.'

The queen came and stood between Katie and Alfie. She put an arm round each of them and hugged them to her. 'All of my children are lovely,' she said.

Just like my kittens, thought Katie with a smile. Tilly, Pebbles, Pixie, Poppy, Suki, Bella and now Ruby. Something told her that with two new babies around, life at the palace was all set to get even more exciting.

☆ Meet a new cute kitten in every adventure! ☆

Pixie
at the Palace

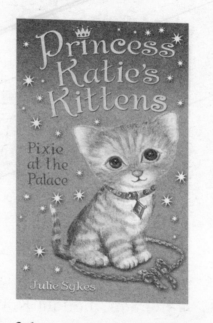

One of the newly found kittens has
gone missing in the woods.
Can Princess Katie and her best friend
Becky find Pixie and bring him
safely back to Starlight Palace?

Bella
at the Ball

Princess Katie is busy preparing for the
queen's magnificent birthday ball, but
Bella is busy getting into mischief! Katie
and Becky must hurry to put things right,
or the whole ball will be ruined!

Poppy
and the Prince

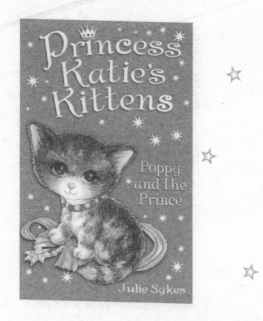

Poppy tries to make friends with Prince
Edward, who thinks cats are silly – but
when the prince gets lost in the palace
maze, it's Poppy who saves the day!

Suki
in the Snow

Suki has crept into Princess Katie's luggage
and has come on her skiing holiday!
But when Suki tries to make her own way
home, Katie and Becky race against time
to find the kitten lost in the snow.

Princess Katie's Kittens

PrincessKatiesKittens.co.uk

Secret facts about the kittens
Kitten puzzles and activities
Princess Katie's top kitten care tips
Book news and more!